The Last of the Unicorns

A Collection

By: Chad Smith

Every word in this book was written by me. No AI was used for ideas or editing.
This comes from the heart.

To find more books by me visit:

www.gattaca.world

Staten House

Intro

I had written this series of poems about a man grieving the death of his horse. I broke it out into four parts.

My wife found it to be a bit too sad for her taste and asked me to write about unicorns.

And so "In the Land of Dead Unicorns" was born.

One day, I thought, "What if the guy mourning his horse was one of the first people to see the unicorns washing up on the beach?"

And so I wrote Coda. Coda will evolve over time, but will probably be the last poem I write. It's time to focus on wrapping up novels.

And as a topic I can't seem to let go...I have a "bonus track" to add to this collection.

Table of Contents

Part One

"Like a fading dream, my horse slips into the eternal pasture."

All the wild horses are standing dead (part 1)

snow is coming

I see their hot breath
    in the icy air

        as they run around the corral

the purple clouds crackle

we set out plates for dinner

    and sit in silence

sometimes

I think you want me to speak

    but I don't

sometimes

I think maybe we could connect

    but my hands feel cold and dead

in the distance

    the rumble of the horses' hooves

All the wild horses are standing dead (part 2)

when you fell
    I was watching
        your brown
            and white
                mane

billowing.

I saw the mud,

    you
        did
            not

the earth shook
    and I knew

    you were not getting
        back up.

I shivered
    cold

as your bones
    broke
        into the ground.

All the wild horses are standing dead (part 3)

that morning
        I woke up
                early

a spinning yellow
        yelp
                as the sun
        peeked

I never open my eyes
        that early

but I wanted to remember
        something
I couldn't grasp

coffee
        eggs
                more yellow

blue flashes
        some wincing
                like lightning

later
        the fall
                the fall

was slow motion
        to me

buckling

I closed my eyes
        no

                        no

                            no

not this.

my eyes burning
            shut

I couldn't breathe

                even at that distance

I felt you leaving me

as I walked *shuffing*

I collapsed on you

                trying

All the wild horses are standing dead (part 4)

you often
      paw me
            in dreams

I am always
      on my back
            in the dirt

in a corral

      the red dust
            stirring the air

you
      so gently

poof
      my shoulder
            with your hoof

and I open
      my eyes

into yours

      as you

            say goodbye.

Part Two

"Unicorns hide not from predators but from a world that has forgotten how to wonder..."

In the Land of Dead Unicorns (part 1)

They wash up onto the beach
pink   and   white   fading
      Horns driven into the sand by the surf
           eyes pale and white

Driven from a faraway island
      some are missing legs
      some are missing their manes
      some bloated and some still dying
Heaving their last breaths
      as jellyfish wash onto the shore to join them

Once they were majestic
      flowing in the wind
           shining in the sun

Now they just rot
      picked apart by seagulls.

In the Land of Dead Unicorns (part 2)

As they wash back out

into the sea

their horns gleam

off the sky

    off the sun

one last farewell.

the green waves

    and white foam

     over them.

In the Land of Dead Unicorns (part 3)

You were always
    dying
        and screaming

but this time
   maybe

the unicorns are all gone now
their brightness faded from the world
the pink and blue
       all grey

I walk through the sand
    hoping to find something
       but feel nothing

for the first time
    in a lifetime
you say kind things
    you love me
       and you are proud of me
          engraved on a cheap watch

and I keep walking
    through the sand
       feeling nothing.

In the Land of Dead Unicorns (part 4)

remnants
      pieces

once again
      floating into the
            white
                sand

we walk down the beach
you so happy
      your red golden retriever floof
         blowing into the wind

once when there were more
      you were so afraid

you find a piece of a neck
mane
      grey in the surf
         and fling it
            with all your might.

In the Land of Dead Unicorns (part 5)

The heat

      we
               set records
                    every day.

Everything seems
      to be dying.

Rain
      a memory of the past.

We go out into the surf
      warm as a hot bath

holding hands

looking for them
      are there any left?

A matted clump of hair
      washes
            over my feet.

I don't know

      from
            what beast

it fell from.

So many bright
      dead things

once floated here

all those years ago.

In the Land of Dead Unicorns (part 6)

so far gone
      (glimpses)
now

our children's children
      no longer believe

they laugh
      at us
            the few who
                  remain

we remember the rumors
      of happiness
            on an island
                 far away

and when they
      finally
arrived

we couldn't believe the news

      but the smell
            miles from the beach

of a million hearts
      breaking at once.

there was no denying

      even still

the sight from
      the boardwalk

into the white sand.

so much ruin
          beautiful

          in death.

Part Three

"Once, they roamed freely, their hooves echoing in forests untouched by sorrow."

Coda

there are days

      when I don't
           remember

but how could I not?

you running to me

      hooves

           trembling

your rush
      pure

the air arriving
      before you

my smiles

      so many years ago

I was lonely

      on Sunday mornings

I walked the beach
      as the tide
           came in

green seas
      warm in-between

                    my toes

sand-playing

          with my toenails

I saw
          the first ones
                    still whole

bellies swollen
          into impossible

sighing
          their last breaths

into
          this world.

Always
          I went to you first

on January mornings

          frost
                    from your nostrils

                    poof
                          in the air

I would bury my head

in your neck
                    you shaking
                          your coarse mane into

                                 my face.

now the snapping
          sound of the surf
takes me from that
          memory

into now.

one
          still alive

thrashing

          trying to swim ashore

the waves
          hurting him

he screams

          I swim out
                    to meet him

so afraid
          that his gleaming horn

          golden in the sun

will tear
          into me

the blue fear
          in his eyes

reminds me

of you

so scared
     after you fell

slipping into the darkness

and your eyes
     knowing

that all the magic in this world
     fades to grey.

Part Four

"The last breath of a unicorn carries with it the whisper of magic fading away."

The Last Unicorn

swam onto the beach
stood up and shook
off all of the salt sea
and then looked around

      for all his fallen people

he had swagger
and threw his horn
gleaming in the sky

after a few steps
into the dry hot
yellow sand
he began to fall

knees trembling
and when his face hit

      he sighed

         sand into the air.

Epilogue

"On the beaches, the unicorn's gentle heart beats one last time."

Acknowledgments

This collection would not have happened without the encouragement of my wife Amiee and my TIRELESS early readers and editors Anastasia Smith, Bryan Center and Andrew Virdin. I love all of you.

About the Author

Chad Smith is a consultant and author hiding out in the Caribbean. He lives with his wife and two neurotic golden retrievers.

www.ingramcontent.com/pod-product-compliance
Lightning Source LLC
Chambersburg PA
CBHW071353130626
46556CB00005B/2159